bindi

BEHIND
THE
SCENES

Dive in Deeper

	DATE DUE		12-12
	FEB 1 0 2013		

Also in the same series:

The Wildlife Games

An Island Escape

A Guest Appearance

BEHIND THE SCENES

Dive in Deeper

Written by Meredith Costain

RANDOM HOUSE AUSTRALIA

1+12

12ᵗᵐ

A Random House book
Published by Random House Australia Pty Ltd
Level 3, 100 Pacific Highway, North Sydney NSW 2060
www.randomhouse.com.au

First published by Random House Australia in 2012

Addresses for companies within the Random House Group can be found at
www.randomhouse.com.au/offices.

National Library of Australia
Cataloguing-in-Publication Entry

Author: Irwin, Bindi, 1998–
Title: Bindi Behind the Scenes: Dive in Deeper /
Bindi Irwin, Meredith Costain
ISBN: 978 1 86471 841 6 (pbk.)
Series: Irwin, Bindi, 1998– Bindi behind the scenes; 4.
Target audience: For primary school age
Other authors/contributors: Costain, Meredith, 1955–
Dewey number: A823.4

Cover photograph © Australia Zoo
Cover and internal design by Christabella Designs
Typeset by Midland Typesetters, Australia
Printed in Australia by Griffin Press, an accredited ISO AS/NZS 14001:2004
Environmental Management System printer

Random House Australia uses papers that are natural, renewable and
recyclable products and made from wood grown in sustainable forests.
The logging and manufacturing processes are expected to conform to the
environmental regulations of the country of origin.

Dear Diary,

I was over the moon when I found out we were going to Lady Elliot Island for our holiday this summer. Who wouldn't be? It's a coral island in the middle of the Great Barrier Reef!

I spent my days snorkelling in the lagoon, soaking up the sunshine on sandy beaches and, best of all, going for a beautiful scuba dive! That meant I could really get up close and personal with some amazing wildlife.

However, my time on the island wasn't all fun and games. I discovered at first hand the terrible things that can happen when people act carelessly and irresponsibly. But I found out some other things about people too. Stuff like how you should never totally give up on someone you think is doing the wrong thing,

because people can change. And how important

trust is between friends – which brings me to life

lesson number four!

true friends are always there for you – whatever, whenever.

Yep, lots of big things happened this past week.

Let me fill you in on the whole story . . .

Bindi

CHAPTER ONE

'I CAN'T BELIEVE IT. WE'RE FLYING through clouds. Not under them or over them, but right *through* them! They look like giant lumps of mashed potato.'

Bindi smiled as Josie pressed her face to the window of the tiny plane. It was hard to miss

the excitement in her friend's voice, even though most of her words were drowned out by the noisy thrum of the engines.

Bindi was excited too. She and her family were on their way to Lady Elliot Island for a well-earned break from their work at Australia Zoo. At the last minute, Josie, her younger brother, Callum, and Josie's mum had decided to come as well. Bindi was looking forward to showing Josie all her favourite parts of the island.

But there was another reason why this particular trip was going to be special. The island was part of the Great Barrier Reef Marine Park. Its clear waters and coral reefs made it the perfect place for scuba diving. Bindi had gone on her first dive when she was 12 and a whole year had passed before she could do it again – she couldn't wait!

The banks of clouds finally gave way to a deep blue sky. 'Is that the island down there?' Josie asked Bindi, pointing to a large dark mass curving beneath them.

'No, that's Fraser Island,' Bindi told her friend. 'Lady Elliot is heaps smaller. You can walk around the whole thing in an hour.'

'And it's shaped just like a turtle, except without any flippers,' Robert Irwin added. 'There it is!' he called, pointing to a tiny speck on the horizon.

The speck grew larger and larger until, finally, it was big enough for Bindi to make out all the things that made the island so special. 'Look, there's the lighthouse and the sandy white beaches, and Coral Gardens, where the dive boats go.' She pointed to an expanse of pale green water rimmed by white-crested breakers. 'And there's the lagoon where we'll go snorkelling.'

'It's beautiful,' sighed Josie.

Bindi grinned. 'Wait till you see what's *inside* the lagoon.'

'Turtles, right?' Josie said. She'd been looking forward to seeing the turtles ever since she'd found out they would be arriving in the middle of the nesting season, when the turtles came out of the ocean to lay their eggs. If they were lucky, they might even see some baby turtles hatch.

'Definitely turtles,' Bindi told her friend. 'And trumpet fish and sea cucumbers and starfish and –'

'Sharks?' a nervous voice asked from the seat behind them.

'It's okay,' said Bindi, turning around to reassure

Callum. 'There *are* lots of reef sharks around the island, but they're pretty harmless. They're more interested in eating fish than people.'

'Yeah, it's two hundred times more likely to be struck by lightning than it is to be attacked by a shark,' Robert chimed in.

'Seriously?' Callum said, his shoulders relaxing. 'That's a relief.'

Bindi gave her brother a wink. She didn't know where he'd pulled that particular fact from, but it seemed to have done the trick.

The little plane banked and turned, then began its descent. The treetops and the cabins of the eco-resort grew closer and closer. A nervous flyer, Josie scrunched her eyes up tight, then opened them as the wheels hit the runway to see a line of waves breaking directly in front of her. Just as she was certain they were all about to end up in the ocean, the plane turned around and headed back down the short runway in the opposite direction, where an identical line of waves stretched ahead. They really were on an island!

She watched from the window as a young woman in an aqua polo shirt and navy shorts waved from the edge of the grass runway.

'Look, Mum,' Bindi said, grabbing her mother's arm. 'It's Nikki!'

Terri smiled. 'Hey, so it is.' She turned around to the rest of the passengers. 'Wave back, everyone. She's welcoming you to the island.'

'Nikki's one of the Activities Officers,' Bindi explained to Josie. 'She knows lots about turtles too. She's doing some research on them for a university in Canada while she's working here.'

'Great,' Josie said, feeling a bit less shaky now that the plane had finally stopped moving.

Everyone collected their hand luggage, then climbed down a set of wobbly metal steps to the ground.

'Welcome to Lady Elliot Island!' Nikki's voice was warm. 'We really hope you're going to enjoy your stay here. If you'd all like to come this way, I'll give you a tour of our facilities.'

She led them down a short path to the entrance to the eco-resort.

'I know some of you have been here before,' she began, sending a special smile in Bindi's direction. Bindi beamed back. 'So you'll already have heard this information. However, there are lots of important things you need to remember

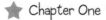

about staying on the island, so I need everyone's full attention, okay?'

Bindi listened dutifully to the instructions about the importance of not crossing the runway if the red light was flashing, and the safe times to go snorkelling in the lagoon. But the whole time she was itching to get to the Dive Shop, to find out more about the times for the scuba diving courses.

Finally, it was time. While Terri helped the boys sort out snorkels, masks and fins from a huge rack on the wall, Bindi and Josie sidled up to the dive counter.

'Hi, Pete,' Bindi said. Pete was one of the diving instructors. He'd been working on the island ever since she could remember.

'Hey, Bindi,' Pete replied, grinning broadly. 'Great to see you guys again. How can I help you?'

'This is my friend Josie. I'd like to sign us both up for the Beginner Scuba Dive Course, please.' Bindi was finding it hard to keep the excitement out of her voice.

'You want to do the Beginner Course again?' Pete asked her, puzzled. 'You picked it all up just fine last time.'

'Thanks,' said Bindi, 'but I thought it would be more fun for Josie if we did the course together. And it won't hurt to have a bit of a refresher, in case I've forgotten anything.'

'Okay then,' Pete said, writing their names in his book, 'two Beginner Scuba Dive Courses it is.' Catching sight of Josie's anxious face, he added, quickly, 'Don't worry, you'll be a natural.'

'You think so?' Josie said shyly.

'Well, if you're anything like your friend here,

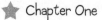

you'll be part-fish already,' Pete teased. 'Right, Bindi?'

'Well, maybe on my left side,' Bindi joked. Bindi loved animals so much, being compared to one was definitely a compliment! 'Seriously, though, I can't wait to dive with Josie.' She looked over to the benches where Robert and Callum were busy choosing snorkels and fins. Snorkelling was great fun, but you could really only stay on the surface of the water. With an air tank on her back, she'd be able to dive deeper and explore all the little caverns and crevices of the reef, on the lookout for fabulous underwater creatures.

It was going to be *amazing*.

CHAPTER TWO

NIKKI LED THE NEW GUESTS on a tour of the resort's facilities. Even though the Irwins had been to the island many times before, they were so happy to be back amongst old friends, they decided to come along for the ride.

'Wow! Look at all the birds,' said Callum, as

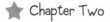

they moved deeper into the gardens. Every branch was full of chattering, squawking and screeching birds.

'It's nesting season,' Nikki explained, 'so there are a lot more birds on the island at the moment. If you look closely at their nests, you'll see most of them have a fuzzy chick inside.'

'They're so noisy,' Josie said, 'but their chicks are cute. And they're so big! Almost the same size as their mums. What sort of birds are they?'

'Noddies,' Nikki told her. 'Anyone want to guess how they got that name?'

'Because they nod their heads up and down a lot?' joked a man who'd been on their flight.

Everyone laughed.

'Actually, that's exactly right,' Nikki told them. 'They've got a long scientific name in Latin as well, but "noddies" is much easier to remember – and spell!' She pointed to a nearby tree. 'Their nests are interesting too, don't you think?'

Callum moved underneath the tree to get a better look.

'Don't get too close,' Bindi warned him, but it was too late. One of the noddies deposited a 'present' on the top of Callum's head.

'Bird poo – gross!' groaned Callum, trying to remove the dollop of sticky white goo from his hair, making an even bigger mess.

'Never mind, Callum,' Terri told him, trying to hide a smile. 'Bird droppings on your head are supposed to be a sign of good luck.'

'Yeah,' giggled Bindi. 'You should have seen how much "good luck" Robert got the first time we came to the island.'

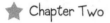

'And now I'm just naturally lucky,' Robert grinned. 'I don't need them anymore.'

The group moved on past the volleyball court and swimming pool, with Callum making sure he stayed well clear of any overhanging branches.

Nikki stopped in front of a giant solar-panel system. 'Most of the power used on the island is produced here,' she told the group, 'and we treat waste in those big tanks over there.' She grinned. 'Actually, nothing gets "wasted" round here – we use the greywater on the gardens, and to irrigate the airstrip. And any leftover food goes into compost pits, which also ends up back in the gardens.'

'What about our drinking and shower water?' Josie's mum, Alison, asked. 'Where does that come from?'

'The ocean! Don't worry,' she said, noticing the

look on Callum's face. 'We take the salt out of it first.'

After a quick tour of the dining room and Education Centre, they finally stopped in front of a row of canvas huts.

'And here's where most of you will be staying for the week,' Nikki told them. She checked her clipboard. 'Bindi, Robert, Josie and Callum? You'll all be in Eco-Cabin Three. Terri and Alison? I've put you in Eco-Cabin Six, a bit further down the row.' She grinned at the two mums. 'I figured the kids might want to have a sleepover.'

'Thanks, Nikki, very thoughtful of you,' Terri said, giving her daughter a wink. 'No wild parties now, do you hear?'

'As if,' laughed Bindi, though secretly she hoped there might be at least one midnight feast during their stay. Normally when they came to the island, the Irwins stayed in one of the family suites. This was the first time she'd been allowed to bunk in with her brother and their friends.

'Okay, I'll leave you all to settle in,' Nikki told them. She checked her watch. 'Don't forget, fish-feeding at 3 pm. Nigel will be waiting for you.'

Puzzled, Josie stared at Bindi as Nikki took the final group of guests off to their cabin. 'Who's Nigel?'

'You'll have to wait and see,' Bindi told her mysteriously. She picked up her bag, then pushed open the door of their eco-cabin. 'Last one in is a rotten egg. And I bags the top bunk.'

'Not if I get there first,' Robert yelped, trying to shove past her.

'And me!' Callum added, joining in the race.

But Bindi and Josie were too quick for them. They both flung their bags on the two top bunks, then scrambled up after them and sat there with their arms circling their knees, guarding their territory.

'Fine,' Robert sighed, sending Callum a meaningful look. 'Have it your way. I just hope you like *hemidactylus frenatus*.'

'What are those?' Josie asked.

'You know, giant lizards with enormous fangs that climb up the walls at night to eat mosquitoes . . . and other things,' Robert said solemnly. He pointed to a spot on the wall, level with Josie's bunk. 'See? Here's a trail one has left behind. Looks like human blood to me.'

'That's it. I'm out of here,' said Josie, clambering

down from the bunk. Callum gave Robert a high-five, then quickly took her place.

Bindi grinned. 'He's joking, Jose. *Hemidactylus frenatus* are geckos which are only about 15 centimetres long, and totally harmless. In fact, they're really quite sweet. They *do* eat mosquitoes though.'

She climbed down to join her friend. 'Okay, here's the deal. Josie and I will share the bunk on this side of the room, and you two can have the other one all to yourselves, complete with geckos. That sound fair?'

'Sure, B, whatever you say,' Robert grinned. He turned to Callum. 'C'mon, Cal, let's go and check out the games room.'

Once the boys were gone, Bindi and Josie unpacked their bags and organised their stuff. It didn't take long. The island was a very casual place with a warm climate all year round, so, apart from their swimming gear, they'd mainly packed things such as T-shirts and shorts.

'I can't believe we're so close to the beach,' Josie said, looking out from the cabin's doorway. The shoreline was only metres away, just the other side of a line of she-oaks. She could hear the waves lapping the sand. 'Normally when we go on holidays, you have to cross a busy highway to get to the beach from your hotel, or pile into the car and drive there.'

'I know,' Bindi said, 'it's one of the things I love about Lady Elliot. And if you come in winter, you can lie on your bed and watch the humpback whales cruising past from Antarctica, on their way to their breeding grounds. You can even hear their songs underwater when you're swimming!'

'Seriously? Then I'm definitely coming back in the winter,' Josie vowed. 'I *love* whales.' She turned to look at the view again. 'Come on, it's too nice outside to stay in here any longer. Besides, I'm itching to see the rest of the island. How about we go for a walk on the beach? Or even a swim?'

'Sure,' said Bindi. 'A swim sounds good to me.'

The girls quickly changed, swapping their travelling clothes for rash vests and board shorts, and applied sunscreen.

'Make sure you wear your reef shoes,' Bindi advised Josie. 'The beaches are covered with old coral and shells, and they can cut your feet if you're not careful.'

Bindi smeared some zinc across her nose and grabbed a shady hat. She was just closing the door when a girl about her age and a slightly older guy came out of the cabin next door to them.

'Ro-ry,' the girl grumbled, 'can't you read?'

'Of course I can read,' the guy answered, breaking into a yawn.

'So why did you leave the light and the fan on?'

Bindi smiled. She knew exactly what their next-door neighbour was talking about. Beside each light switch in every cabin on the island was a sticker with a little picture of a turtle and a polite request to turn off all lights and fans when exiting the room. The people who ran the eco-resort were working really hard to show people how important it was not to waste our planet's natural resources – not just on the island, but everywhere. Electrical

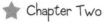

appliances and lights needed energy to work, and all that energy had to come from somewhere.

The guy rolled his eyes. 'Because it's hot in there. I figured if I left the fan going the room would be cool by the time we came back.'

'But that's such a waste of power. Anyway, fans make *you* cool, not the room. How are they going to do that if we're not even in there? And leaving the light on definitely isn't going to make the room any cooler.'

'Okay already, I'll go back in and turn them off,' the guy muttered. 'Who made you the boss all of a sudden?' Dumping his towel on a deckchair by the door, he stomped back inside.

Realising their little argument had been overheard, the girl gave Bindi and Josie an apologetic look. 'Sorry about my brother. He can be a real pain sometimes.'

Josie smiled at her. 'Don't worry about it. I know all about brothers. Mine's younger than yours, but he's probably just as annoying.'

'A few days on the island will cheer him up,' Bindi assured the girl, pleased to see a shared passion for helping to look after the planet. 'And once he sees all the beautiful creatures here, I'm sure he'll go out of his way to do everything he can to help protect them.' She grinned. 'I'm Bindi, by the way, and this is my friend Josie.'

The girl stared at her. 'Bindi – as in Bindi Irwin from Australia Zoo?'

'That's me. How did you know?'

'We visited your zoo last year for my birthday,' the girl told Bindi. 'I love animals too. I'm always reading about them or watching nature documentaries on TV. I saw you and your brother doing the crocodile-feeding show in the Croc-oseum. And I joined up to be a Wildlife Warrior after the talk you gave.'

'Fantastic,' Bindi said. 'The world's wildlife needs all the help it can get. What's your name?'

'Jasmine, but everyone just calls me Jaz.'

'Except me,' interrupted her brother, who'd returned. 'I call her –'

Jaz glared at her brother, then jumped in quickly before he revealed his embarrassing nickname for her. 'Rory, this is Bindi Irwin from Australia Zoo. Remember? We went there last year.'

Rory stopped teasing his sister and turned to face Bindi and Josie. He was actually kind of cute, Bindi decided, especially his eyes, which were the same colour green as the water on the outer reef.

It was a pity he had such bad habits when it came to energy conservation.

Rory scratched his head. 'Let me think . . . The place with the big crocs?'

'That's the one,' Bindi laughed. 'Though we have lots of other wild animals from all around the world. Tigers and cheetahs, rhinos, red pandas, and –'

'Crocodiles,' said Rory. 'Sure, I remember now.' He picked up his towel again. 'So are we going to the beach still?' he asked his sister. 'Or did you want to stay here and chat to your new friends?'

'We were just about to go to the beach too,' Bindi said. 'I promised to show Josie my favourite one, near the lighthouse, round the other side of the island. Maybe we could all go together?'

'Fine with me,' Jaz said, her face lighting up. 'Sounds like you've been here before. We just arrived this morning, so we haven't had much of a chance to look around yet. Want to lead the way?'

'Absolutely,' Bindi said, pleased with the way things were working out. She'd only been on the island for a few hours and she'd already signed up for her dive lesson, met a whole new clutch of noddy chicks and made some new friends. 'Follow me.'

CHAPTER THREE

BINDI LED JOSIE AND THEIR neighbours through the gardens and onto the narrow white beach that ran in front of the resort.

'We'll head up this way,' Bindi told them. 'It's quicker to go across the airstrip and through the Bird Rookery, but the view is so much nicer from

the beach. And by the time we get there, we'll have walked halfway around the island!'

While they walked, the group chatted about where everyone came from and their reasons for visiting Lady Elliot. Jaz and Rory lived in Queensland too, but further down the coast from Bindi and Josie. They'd caught a plane from a different airport that morning and had enjoyed their flight through the clouds as well.

'My mum's a biologist, who specialises in plankton,' Jaz explained. 'She's meeting up with some other researchers here for a kind of mini-conference. And Dad's an engineer, but he's on leave at the moment, so he's signed up to help out with Project Manta while we're here.'

'What's Project Manta?' Josie asked.

'It's this group of scientists who are studying

manta rays,' Jaz explained. 'They're collecting information on stuff like how many there are, how long they live for and where they go when they're not hanging around the island. But anyone can help out with the research. They ask all the divers who come here to post any photos they take on their website.'

'Mantas are amazing,' said Bindi. 'They're *so* big. Bigger than cars – or even caravans! They have really wide mouths and each one has a unique pattern of markings on their belly, just like a fingerprint.'

'Exactly, and that's how researchers identify them,' Jaz said, nodding. 'They even give them names, like Spotty or Nautilus. Dad's going to help out by taking photos of mantas he sees while we're here. He borrowed a special underwater camera from one of his mates.'

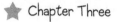

'So your dad knows how to scuba dive?' Bindi asked.

'He used to dive when he was younger,' Jaz said. 'He's going to do a refresher course first before he goes out with the team.'

'How about you guys?' Bindi asked. 'Do you dive too?'

'Not yet, but we will soon. We've both signed up for the Beginner Scuba Dive Course.'

'So have we!' Bindi said. 'When's your first lesson?'

'Wednesday morning,' Jaz said. 'They already had a big group booked in for tomorrow.'

'Same!' Bindi cried. 'We'll all be diving together. And tomorrow, we can all go snorkelling in the lagoon, and –' She broke off, realising her new friends might already have other plans.

'Well, that's if you want to, of course,' she added shyly.

'Absolutely,' Jaz said. 'It sounds like fun. Rory? What do you reckon?'

Rory shrugged. 'May as well. Nothing else to do round here.'

Bindi stared at him. Was he joking? There never seemed to be enough hours in the day to fit in all the things she wanted to do on the island. Snorkelling, reef walking and beachcombing, plus there was always something interesting going on in the Education Centre. Sometimes they even had a visiting scientist give a lecture, or they showed wildlife documentaries about the local marine environment.

'Rory's only interested in playing online computer games with his friends,' Jaz said. 'I'm

surprised his eyes haven't gone square, he spends so much time in front of a screen.'

'Except I can't play, can I?' Rory whinged. 'It's like being grounded.' His parents had refused to buy him any internet vouchers, saying it wouldn't hurt him to go without for a few days. 'And there's no mobile-phone reception. Whoever heard of that? I can't even call my mates to find out what they've been up to.'

'Hello?' his sister said. 'We're on a tiny island in the middle of the ocean? It's a bit far for the signals to reach, don't you think?'

'Then they should build bigger towers,' Rory said, reaching down to pick up a shell. He studied it for a while, then slipped it into his pocket.

Bindi and Jaz exchanged looks.

'What?' Rory said. 'Aren't I allowed to pick

up shells now? I just wanted it for a souvenir.'

'You can pick them up, sure,' Bindi told him. 'You just can't take them away with you.'

'Says who?'

'Lady Elliot Island is in a Green Zone,' Bindi explained patiently. 'That means everything on it is protected.'

'Living things, sure, I get that,' Rory countered. 'Birds and fish and turtles and stuff. But a shell isn't a living thing. It's just a shell.'

'But it can be a home for a living thing,' Bindi told him. 'In this case, it's more like a mobile home. Hermit crabs don't have hard shells to protect the soft parts of their bodies like other crabs do.'

'Really?' Josie said. 'I never knew that.'

Bindi nodded. 'The only way they can survive

is to find empty shells on the beach and use those instead. They don't just stay in the same one either – they have to keep finding bigger and bigger ones as they grow. That's why it's really important you don't take them away from the beach. Imagine if every tourist who came here wanted to take home a souvenir with them!'

'Okay, okay, I get the message.' Rory took the shell out of his pocket and placed it back on the beach, then picked up a knobbly piece of sun-bleached coral. 'What about this? There's heaps of it. Nobody's going to miss one piece, or even five hundred pieces.'

Bindi shook her head. 'Same deal. There's a saying on the island: "Take away nothing but awesome memories".'

'Hey, that's a good one,' Jaz said. 'I'm going to

remember that next time I see people taking stuff from our local park. They're always picking flowers or collecting fallen branches and twigs for firewood. Maybe some of those branches are homes for other types of animals.'

Sighing, Rory put the piece of coral back where he'd found it. 'I told you this place was boring,' he grumbled, mopping his face with his towel. 'Have we reached your beach yet, Bindi? I'm dying for a swim.'

'It's just around the next headland, beyond those rocks,' Bindi said. 'Just watch out where you put your feet,' she called after Rory, who'd begun to race ahead. 'Lots of gulls nest along the shoreline here. They're very protective of their eggs!'

But it was too late. A flock of gulls descended on Rory, swooping at his head.

'Get these crazy birds away from me!' he shouted, waving his arms around.

Bindi sighed. Rory might be cute, but he knew nothing about animal behaviour. His sister was right. He needed to spend less time in front of a screen and more time in the real world.

'Just walk away quietly,' she advised him, 'this way, towards the water. Once they see you're not going to go after their chicks or eggs, they'll leave you alone.'

Red-faced, Rory rejoined the others.

Minutes later, Bindi and her friends were splashing around in the warm waters of the Great Barrier Reef Marine Park. Schools of colourful fish darted past their legs, while flocks of gulls and terns wheeled overhead.

Who needs the internet or mobile phones when

you can have all this? Bindi thought as she floated on her back, staring up at the endless blue sky. It was her idea of heaven.

CHAPTER FOUR

THE NEXT MORNING, AFTER A
huge breakfast, Bindi took Josie over to the pool
for her snorkelling lesson. They'd arranged to meet
up with Jaz and Rory there, but so far only Jaz had
turned up.

'Where's Rory?' Bindi asked.

'Still sleeping,' Jaz answered, shrugging.

'You're joking,' said Bindi, who'd been up since dawn. She loved watching the sun rising over the lagoon. 'But it's such a beautiful day!'

'He was up late watching some video in the rec room,' said Jaz. 'Guess he needed his TV fix.'

By now, a group of other guests had assembled by the pool. After a few minutes, Nikki joined them. Greeting new arrivals to the island was only one of her many jobs. 'Morning, everyone!' she announced brightly. 'How are we all today? Ready to get wet?'

The guests, who came from all over the world, nodded and smiled.

'Okay, let's go over to the Dive Shop so we can get your gear organised.'

As they walked the short distance from the pool,

Nikki fell into step beside Bindi and her friends. 'We missed you at the fish-feeding yesterday,' she told Bindi. 'Nigel especially.'

Bindi laughed. 'Yeah, sorry about that. I took everyone round to Coral Gardens for a swim. We kind of lost track of time.'

Josie tugged Bindi's arm. 'Who is this Nigel?' she insisted. 'How come you've never told me about him?'

Nikki and Bindi exchanged amused smiles.

'She hasn't?' Nikki said, her eyes dancing. 'I find that hard to believe. He's *very* attractive.'

'Very,' Bindi agreed mysteriously.

'So when can I meet him?' Josie asked.

'Yeah, I want to meet him too,' Jaz agreed, as they reached the Dive Shop. 'He sounds –'

'Jaz!' a voice called. 'Wait up.'

The girls spun around to see Rory loping towards them, still half-asleep. His T-shirt looked like he'd slept in it, and a lock of blond hair was sticking straight up from the back of his head.

'About time,' Jaz sighed, rolling her eyes. 'You almost missed the lesson.'

Now that everyone had arrived, Nikki swung into action, working with the Dive Shop team to make sure everyone had suitable gear.

She handed Josie a pair of fins. 'These look about your size,' she said, showing Josie how to fit them snugly around her heel. 'Okay, now for the mask. Make sure it's nice and tight. We don't want any water to get in.'

Josie put the plastic mask over her eyes and nose and adjusted the straps. 'Like this?' she asked Nikki.

'Perfect. Now, there are three things you need to know about snorkelling gear. Don't let any strands of hair get under the mask or it will break the seal and let water in. Breathe through your mouth instead of your nose. And most importantly, don't smile!'

Josie grinned. The last instruction was impossible. How could you stop yourself from smiling when someone has just told you not to do it!

As soon as everyone was kitted out, Nikki led them back to the swimming pool so they could try out their gear before hitting the ocean for the first time.

Bindi watched from the side as one by one they used their fins to help propel them across the surface of the pool, all the while keeping their faces in the water. Jaz and Rory picked it up quickly, but

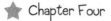

Josie seemed to be struggling. After a few attempts she moved back to the shallow end of the pool and stood there, fiddling with her mask.

'You okay, Jose?' Bindi called to her friend.

Josie shook her head. 'Not really.'

'Hang on, I'm coming over.' Bindi scooted round to the other side of the pool until she was right next to Josie. 'What's wrong?'

Josie pulled a face. 'I can't get the breathing right and my mask keeps fogging up. And water's coming down the snorkel and into my mouth.'

'Just take little breaths. In and out like this,' Bindi advised, demonstrating what she meant.

Josie tried to copy what she was doing, but it didn't seem to make any difference. 'It's no good. I'm hopeless. I can't do it.'

'Yes, you can,' Bindi assured her. 'You're trying too hard. Just relax and breathe naturally.'

Josie tried again, but the taste of the rubbery mouthpiece made her feel sick. If she didn't take it out of her mouth, she was going to throw up, like, right now! She ripped off the mask and snorkel, then hauled herself out of the water onto the edge of the pool. 'I might as well go back to the cabin,' she sighed, as Jaz swam over to join them.

'This snorkelling stuff is easy-peasy,' she began, then stopped when she saw Josie's white face. 'Everything okay?'

'She's fine,' Bindi said quickly. 'Just swallowed a bit of water, didn't you, Jose?' Before Josie could answer, Bindi pointed to the other side of the pool, where Nikki was rounding everyone up for the

next stage of the lesson. 'Looks like we're ready to do the real thing.'

'Great!' Jaz said. 'I can't wait.'

After Jaz had left the pool, Bindi moved closer to her friend. 'Lots of people have trouble with the breathing the first time they try snorkelling,' she said. 'It's nothing to worry about. I'll help you practise some more this afternoon.'

'But if I can't do it, I'm going to miss out on all the fun this morning,' Josie said, unable to keep the disappointment out of her voice. Everyone in the group was going off on a trip in a glass-bottomed boat to the part of the reef near the lighthouse. The water there was really deep, and they'd be able to see lots of different marine life, including turtles. While she'd be able to see turtles and fish through the glass, Josie knew it wouldn't be the same as actually being in the water with them.

And there was another problem. If she couldn't get the breathing right, how would she ever be able to dive? Breathing with a regulator and an air tank, deep below the surface, was a lot more complicated than using a snorkel. Bindi would go off with Jaz and Rory, and she'd be left all on her own.

'Hey, hurry up, you guys!' Jaz called, waving at them from the pool gate. 'Nikki says we're leaving for the boat trip in two minutes.'

'C'mon, Josie,' Bindi said. 'Who knows? We might see some manta rays!'

'Okay,' Josie replied, smiling at her friend. Bindi was always so enthusiastic about anything to do with animals, it was hard not to get caught up in it. 'I guess I can do that.'

Ten minutes later, after a speedy trip across the island on the back of a truck, the snorkelling group waded out through knee-high swirling water and clambered onto the deck of the boat. As the boat picked up speed, everyone moved closer to the glass panels so they could see what was going on in the underwater world beneath them. They gasped at the sight of shoals of colourful fish playing hide-and-seek through waving fronds of algae and seagrass.

'Look!' said Bindi, pointing to a large creature resting on a rock below. 'I've just spotted our first turtle!'

'Where? Where?' came the cries, as people jostled each other to get a better look. Several of the other members of the group pulled out cameras so they could take some snaps.

'It looked like it was sleeping,' Josie said, as the boat moved to another part of the reef. 'Do turtles sleep?'

'Sure, but only for a few hours at a time,' Bindi explained. 'They breathe air just like we do. When they're swimming and eating, they have to come up to the surface every few minutes or so to breathe.' She pointed off to the left side of the boat. 'Just like that one's doing now, see?'

Everyone with a camera quickly turned away from the glass panels and started clicking madly as a young turtle swam past them, its head and neck curving out of the water as it gulped down a few breaths of air. Then it dived down under the surface again, only to reappear a few minutes later even closer to the boat.

'Hey, I think he likes us!' Josie said. 'But what

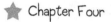

about that one we saw on the bottom? Is it okay? Doesn't it have to come up for air too?'

'Don't worry, it's perfectly fine,' Bindi assured her. 'When they're in a resting state, they can stay underwater for two or three hours at a time. They seem to be able to store oxygen in their bodies better than other animals. At least, mature turtles can. The young ones sleep while they're floating on the surface.'

'Clever,' Jaz said. 'Much cleverer than people. And we're going to get to swim with them!' She turned towards Josie. 'I can't wait for our diving lesson, can you?'

'Nope,' Josie muttered, trying to put on her bravest smile. 'Can't wait.'

CHAPTER FIVE

BINDI FILLED HER PLATE AT THE

buffet and brought it over to the table she was

sharing with her friends. The food was yet another

reason why Bindi loved the island – the meals

were awesome! The lunchtime buffet was always

popular, with a hot food bar of stir fries and pasta,

bowls of crunchy salads, flat bread to make your own wraps, and platters of juicy tropical fruit.

Rory joined her at the table, his plate piled high with food.

Jaz looked at the mountain of chips on his plate and smiled. 'Feeling a little hungry?'

'Just a bit,' he grinned back, squeezing tomato sauce all over his lunch.

'It's the fresh air and salt water,' Bindi said. 'Plus all that swimming.'

'Yeah, he's actually doing something for a change, rather than watching other people on TV,' Jaz teased. She heaped a pile of chicken strips and salad onto a piece of flat bread, squirted it with mayo, rolled it up, then took a huge bite.

'Now who's the hungry one?' her brother teased back.

'Can you believe some of the things we saw out on the reef?' Jaz said, ignoring him. 'Clams, sea anemones and those bright blue sea stars. And some yellow and blue fish swam past and tickled my legs. I saw six turtles too!'

'Only six?' Rory said. 'I saw at least eight. And a shark.' He held his arms out wide. 'It was *this* big!'

'Actually, I think it was just a grouper,' Jaz corrected him. She turned to Josie, who was quietly eating a bowl of salad. 'That's a type of fish,' she explained.

'Really,' Josie said tightly, staring into her bowl. She'd seen some of the things they were describing, through the glass panels on the bottom of the boat. But she'd spent most of the time taking a zillion photos for an elderly American couple

who couldn't work out how to use their camera. 'It sounds amazing.'

'Next time it will be you out there too, Josie,' Bindi said kindly. She took a bite of her wrap and chewed it thoughtfully. 'So, guys, what are we going to do this afternoon?'

'There are a few more DVDs in the rec room I haven't seen yet,' Rory suggested.

'No way,' scoffed Jaz. 'Mum says I have to make sure you spend the day *outside*, not lolling around on a couch.' She reached over to an empty table next to them and grabbed the list of activities on offer for the day. 'Let's see. We could go on the Bird Watching Tour or a guided reef walk. Anyone want to do either of those?'

'Who needs to go on a tour to see birds?' Rory said. 'They're everywhere. You can't miss them.'

'Yes, but you can find out more about them,' Bindi said. 'Where they've come from and where they're off to next. Some of them have flown for thousands of kilometres to get here. Or we could take the Climate Change Tour and find out why so many of the island's trees are dying and why the reef's in trouble.

'Scientists reckon that one third of the carbon dioxide produced every time you start a car or turn on a light is absorbed by the ocean, which makes it more acidic. All that acid is making the coral and shells brittle and weak, which slows down their growth. If we're not careful, one day we might lose the reef altogether.'

'See, Rory,' Jaz said. 'I told you it was important to turn off the lights when you're not using them.'

Rory rolled his eyes. 'I'll remember that next

time you're using your hair straightener. What a waste of energy *that* is!'

'Well, at least I don't spend half an hour in the shower every day like you do.'

Bindi and Josie exchanged looks. They both had little brothers that liked to tease them occasionally, but they never argued with them like these two.

'So, guys,' Bindi jumped in, 'we still haven't decided what we're going to do.'

Josie picked up the list and scanned it quickly. 'How about the Island Tucker Tour? They show you how to find plants on the island that can be used for food or medicine.'

'Hey, that would be perfect for you,' Bindi said. Josie was the most amazing cook. Whenever Bindi visited her friend's house, Josie was always whipping up a batch of decorated cupcakes or yummy things like French toast with local macadamia nuts and maple syrup. 'What do you think, Jaz? The tour starts in half an hour.'

Jaz wrinkled her nose. 'Doesn't really sound like my kind of thing,' she said. 'I'd rather do something with animals than plants.' She twirled her long ponytail with her fingers for a moment. 'Hey, I know, why don't you go off and do the Island Tucker Tour, Josie, and Bindi, you and Rory and I can go snorkelling again. Maybe this time we *will* see a shark.'

Fat chance, Josie thought, as Jaz chattered on and on about the different types of sharks on the island, showing off how knowledgeable she was. There was no way she was going to get left out of things a second time. It had been bad enough being stuck on the boat all morning.

Meanwhile, Bindi thought hard. There had to be something they could do that would keep everyone happy. 'I know,' she said, brightening. 'Why don't we just do our own tour of the island? So far you've only seen the beaches, but there's heaps to see inland as well. We could start at the entrance to the Bird Rookery, check out the fruit on the Pisonia trees in the gardens, then visit the graveyard –'

'There's a graveyard?' Rory said. 'Awesome.'

'Sure is. After that we can check out the lighthouse, and Ben's Beach Hut –'

'Who's Ben?' Jaz asked. 'Is he a friend of Nigel's?'

'Maybe, maybe not,' Bindi teased her. 'He's very –' She broke off as she noticed a small brown bird at her feet. 'Hello, Jackson,' she said, surprised but happy to see him. 'Wow, you've grown!'

Jackson fixed her with a beady eye, then went back to pecking at the carpet.

'You know this bird?' Rory asked, surprised she could tell one bird from the thousands of others on the island. As far as he was concerned, they all looked the same.

'Sure, we made friends the last time we stayed here.' Bindi turned back to Jackson. 'Didn't we, little mate?'

'Aww, he's so sweet,' Jaz said, as he fluttered up from the floor to the table. 'I wish I had a pet bird like him.'

Josie saw a chance to turn Bindi's attention away from Jaz and back to her. Breaking off a piece from her bread roll, she held it out to the tiny bird.

'Come here, Jackson,' she coaxed, moving her hand closer to his beak. 'Look what I've got for you.'

Bindi quickly reached across and took the piece of bread before Jackson could swallow it. Startled, Josie drew back, causing Jackson to flutter away to try his luck at another table.

'Sorry, Jose, I didn't mean to frighten you,' she said. 'It's just that it's not a good idea to feed bread to birds. It's like giving them their version of junk food – there's no goodness in it for them.'

'Yeah,' Jaz chimed in. 'And if they get too dependent on it, they'll stop looking for the kind of food that *would* be good for them. Plus dry bread might swell up in their insides and cause a blockage.' She paused. 'It might even kill them.'

Bindi smiled at her new friend. 'You really do know a lot about wildlife.'

'Thanks,' Jaz said, chuffed. 'I'm thinking of studying zoology when I finish school.'

'Really?' Bindi said. 'Hey, maybe you can get a job at Australia Zoo. We might even end up working together. Wouldn't that be awesome!'

Josie stared at the floor, her cheeks burning. Instead of making things better between herself and her old friend, she'd just made them worse! Now Bindi was going to think she was a klutz who gave birds bad habits, when really she loved animals. She just didn't go round talking about them all the time like Jaz did.

'Okay, so it's all decided then?' said Bindi, gathering up their dishes. 'We'll do our own island tour and be back at the lagoon in time for the fish-feeding.'

'Sounds good to me,' Jaz said. She flicked at an imaginary bit of grot on the front of her T-shirt. 'Should I change my top in case Nigel brings a friend?'

'He'll probably bring heaps,' Bindi said, enjoying the mystery she was creating.

'Even better!' Jaz laughed.

'Maybe one of them will have a phone with reception,' Rory said hopefully.

'I doubt it,' Bindi said, pushing her chair back from the table. 'And, Jaz, you look perfectly fine how you are. C'mon, everyone. Let's go!'

CHAPTER SIX

BINDI AND HER FRIENDS EMERGED

from the Rookery, amazed by the number of sea
birds nesting there. The sound of tens of thousands
of noddies and gulls chattering and calling to
each other had been almost deafening. It was
hard to imagine how quiet the island would be

once the birds moved on to other parts of the world.

The group rounded a bend in the path and bumped into a bunch of kids carrying walking poles and sea scopes.

'Hey, little buddy,' Bindi greeted her brother, who'd been reef walking with the Reef Rangers club on the outer rim of the coral cay. 'Seen any giant flesh-eating geckos on your travels?'

'Hey, B,' Robert replied with a grin. 'No geckos this time. We saw plenty of leopard sea cucumbers though. Does that count? And Callum reckons he saw a cone shell in a tide pool.'

'I hope you didn't pick it up,' Bindi said, alarmed. Cone shells were a really dangerous type of marine snail. They had venomous little harpoons on their tongues that could kill a fish in less than a second!

'It's okay,' Robert assured her. 'The first thing Chloe did when we started our reef walk was to warn everyone not to touch or step on any marine creatures, especially anything shaped like a cone.'

'Yeah, she kept saying "look but don't touch" every five minutes,' Callum added.

'Good,' Bindi said, relieved. It was a long way back to the mainland if anyone needed emergency medical treatment. 'So where are you guys off to now?'

'Can't say,' Robert replied. 'It's a secret. Anyway, we better go catch up with the others, or we'll get left behind.'

'Okay, see you at dinner!'

'Your family is full of secrets,' Jaz sighed, once

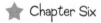

the boys had gone. Jaz turned to the group. 'So where are *we* off to next?'

'The graveyard,' Bindi said. 'It's just along this path.'

'Cool,' said Rory, unscrewing the cap of a bottle of mineral water.

He drank the last of the water, then hurled the bottle over his shoulder into the bushes.

The three girls stared at him in horror.

'Rory!' Jaz thundered. 'Go over there and pick that up!'

Rory wrinkled his nose. 'It's just a water bottle.' He pointed to the thick vegetation surrounding the path. 'Look, you can't even see it anymore. It's not like anyone's going to trip over it or anything.'

'But it's made of plastic,' Bindi pointed out. 'And it's bound to end up in the ocean eventually.

Just like all those bottles that people drop in the street, because they can't be bothered trying to find a recycling bin. They roll into the gutter and get washed down storm drains, then out to sea.'

'So? They'll probably just float around for a bit and then break down,' Rory said. He yawned. 'The sun's so hot up here, that shouldn't take too long.'

Bindi was about to tell him why that was never going to happen, then decided it was best to do it back at the eco-resort, where she could use the information and pictures in the Education Centre to help to get her message across.

It actually took hundreds of years for the plastic used for water bottles and grocery bags to break down. And the molecules in plastic never 'disappeared' completely – they just broke down into smaller and smaller pieces. During Bindi's last visit to the island, the Education Centre had screened a documentary about the dangers of plastics to sea turtles and other marine animals. She had learnt about the millions of little bits and pieces of plastic floating around in the ocean that had come together to form a kind of island of 'plastic soup' known as the Great Pacific Garbage Patch. It covered an area about the same size as New South Wales and was six metres deep. Bindi couldn't even begin to imagine how many plastic items had been thrown out to make such a huge mess.

It was sad to think about the hundreds of thousands of sea birds and animals that died every year after getting themselves tangled in the plastic or swallowing it. Turtles, she'd discovered, often mistook plastic shopping bags for jellyfish, one of their favourite foods. The bags then lodged in their intestines, blocking their digestive systems and sometimes causing them to die from starvation.

Bindi particularly remembered the part of the documentary about a very sick green sea turtle in Florida. The vets who had treated it had found 74 different pieces of man-made material inside it. Not just pieces of plastic, although there were plenty of those, but balloons and pieces of string! Maybe if she told Rory about the turtle and showed him photos, it might make him act a bit more responsibly about littering.

'Is that the graveyard over there? It's not very big.' Jaz's voice brought her hurtling back to the present.

Bindi followed Jaz's gaze to a small group of headstones surrounded by rambling flowers and a picket fence. 'Not many people lived here before the resort was built,' she explained. 'It was mainly just the lighthouse keepers. There've been lots of shipwrecks though.'

Josie moved closer to the headstones so she could read the names and dates on them. 'I love imagining the stories behind the names,' she said. 'You know, who the people were and what their lives and families were like. Even how they died.'

'You should be a writer,' Bindi said, smiling at her friend.

Josie blushed. She'd never told Bindi this, but being a writer was *exactly* what she wanted to do. She was always scribbling thoughts and stories down in secret notebooks when no-one was looking.

'Maybe we should come back at midnight and

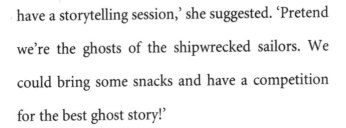

have a storytelling session,' she suggested. 'Pretend we're the ghosts of the shipwrecked sailors. We could bring some snacks and have a competition for the best ghost story!'

Jaz rolled her eyes. 'Maybe if I was 10 years old, at a sleepover. I grew out of telling ghost stories years ago.'

Josie stared at her, crushed. Why did Jaz have to say it like that? It wasn't like she'd ever done anything to upset her.

'Aw-kward . . .' Rory muttered, not helping the situation.

'Let's have one when we get back home,' Bindi said quickly, sensing the tension in the air. She grinned. 'Anyway, I've got other plans for tonight – plans I think you're all going to like.'

'Do they involve Nigel?' Jaz asked, perking up.

'Not this time,' Bindi laughed. She checked her watch. 'Though I'm glad you reminded me. It's almost time for the fish-feeding. Come on, if we take a short cut across the airstrip, we should make it just in time.'

And after that, she'd tell Rory about the Florida turtle. Maybe hearing something like that would make him think twice about dropping litter wherever he felt like it. Then again, maybe not. Sometimes people had to see stuff for themselves to really understand it.

CHAPTER SEVEN

BY THE TIME THEY REACHED THE
Fish Pool, Nikki had already begun feeding
the fish. Bindi and her friends joined the other
guests standing in the shallow water, as groups
of different-coloured fish swarmed around their
ankles.

'Hey, that tickles,' Jaz giggled, as a school of tiny fish began nibbling at her left foot. 'The food's over that way.'

'Sounds like you've just had a visit from some cleaner wrasse,' Nikki told her. 'Have you got any cuts or nicks on your feet?'

'Sure do,' Jaz said. A piece of coral had grazed her ankle during their beach walk the day before. It had hurt a bit at the time, but she'd forgotten all about it. Until now! She pulled her foot out of the water, worried the fish might take this biting thing a bit too far.

'Don't worry,' Nikki reassured her, 'they're just trying to clean you up.' She turned to the rest of the group. 'Anyone see the movie *Shark Tale*?'

Most of the guests raised their hands.

'Remember the car-wash scene, when the big fish

parked themselves so they could get cleaned up by the little cleaner fish? Well, that's kind of what's going on here, except without the sponges and buckets of bubbly shampoo. In deeper parts of the reef, sharks and manta rays line up and wait for their turn to be cleaned. The cleaner wrasse nibble away at the dead skin and parasites on their skin or inside their mouths – it's like their dinner! So everyone's happy.'

Noticing the horrified look on Jaz's face at the mention of parasites, she added quickly, 'Not that they'd be looking for bugs on *human* feet! So you don't need to worry about that.'

'Phew!' Jaz laughed.

Throwing another handful of microalgae into the lagoon from her bucket, Nikki continued her talk, pointing out the different types of fish that had turned up for their daily treat.

'So, here we have some sergeant majors,' she said, pointing to a school of pretty, blue and green banded fish. 'The bigger fish over there are Moses perch. Oh, and look, here come some moon wrasse.'

'They're so pretty,' said a little girl, watching the group of blue, pink and purple fish. She held out her hand for some of the fish food. 'Can I help you feed them?'

Nikki shook her head. 'Sorry, sweetheart, only staff are allowed to feed the fish. The island has to operate under strict rules that protect the fish, and we have to be very careful not to give them too much food. They might stop looking for their own food if they knew they could always get enough here in the Fish Pool. You wouldn't want that to happen, would you?'

The little girl shook her head solemnly, making the other guests laugh.

Nikki turned back to the group. 'Moon wrasse are very clever,' she continued. 'They can change their sex. They all start out as female but can become male.'

'That would be *so* weird,' Josie whispered. 'Imagine waking up one morning and discovering you'd turned into a guy overnight!'

'Eew, gross,' Jaz agreed. 'You'd suddenly have to do boy stuff like playing endless games of World of Warcraft, or wearing the same T-shirt and socks for a week.'

Bindi was about to add a few more things to the list – like having an obsession with cars – when Rory grabbed Jaz's arm, making her jump. 'Hey, looks like we're going to be on TV!'

Bindi spun round. A camera crew were setting up on the beach behind them, chattering away in a foreign language. She wasn't entirely sure which language it was, but it sounded like Japanese. A few years ago, she'd spent a couple of weeks in Japan visiting her friend Emi, helping her to photograph a group of snow monkeys. She'd learnt to speak a few phrases, such as *'arigato'*, which meant 'thank you', and *'Konnichiwa, ogenki desu ka'*, which meant 'Hello, how are you?'. But not enough to be able to work out why the camera crew were there.

'Maybe they're filming us for the news,' Jaz said, smoothing out her wind-rumpled hair with her fingers. 'All my friends will see us.'

'Only if your friends have moved to Japan,' said Rory.

Bindi smiled, pleased that her initial guess had

been correct. Her mum was always telling her she had a good ear for languages, which was going to come in very handy if she was to continue her work travelling around the world as a Wildlife Warrior. 'Do you speak Japanese?' she asked Rory.

'A little bit,' he told her. 'Some of my gaming friends come from Japan. We chat on Skype all the time. You kind of pick up stuff after a while.'

Jaz gave her brother a playful push. 'So all your game-playing finally turned out to be good for something after all. Go and find out what they're doing here,' she urged him.

Bindi shook her head, signalling that she thought that was a bad idea. Nikki's bucket would be close to empty by now, and the rest of the guests were starting to drift away. Rather than interrupt the crew, who were busy doing a piece to camera, Bindi decided it would be better to ask Nikki about them instead. She always seemed to know everything about everything!

Sure enough, Nikki knew exactly what was going on. The camera crew were from Japan, Rory had been right about that. They were travelling around Australia making a TV series about Australian animals. So far they'd been down south to Victoria, filming platypuses and kangaroos, and north to Kakadu to observe crocodiles. Now they'd come to Lady Elliot Island to film the amazing creatures of the Great Barrier Reef.

'You'd better get used to them,' Nikki laughed. 'They're going to be here all week.'

'Doesn't bother me,' said Jaz, wishing she was wearing a better T-shirt than the old baggy one she'd thrown on that morning. She loved acting in school productions and dreamt of being discovered by a talent scout. She'd only really thought about getting a role in a family drama or a popular show such as *Home and Away*. But something with animals in it, like the show the Japanese crew were filming, would be perfect!

Nikki looked at Bindi thoughtfully. 'Maybe I should let them know you and your family are staying here, Bindi,' she suggested. 'I'm sure they'd love to interview you for the show.'

Bindi smiled. 'No, that's okay, Nikki. This is supposed to be our holiday, remember? We do plenty of that kind of stuff the rest of the year. Besides, I'm going to be too busy for interviews once I start diving again. You won't be able to keep me out of the water!'

'Too busy to go turtle trekking tonight?' Nikki

asked her. 'I'm just going over to the office to set up for the briefing. You guys should all come. Plus there's a special someone there I know you'd love to meet.'

Josie's ears pricked up. 'Nigel?' she asked hopefully, as Nikki headed off to the Education Centre. 'Bindi, I thought you said we'd meet him at the fish-feeding?'

Bindi shrugged. 'I thought so too. Looks like he didn't show, but I'm sure we'll meet him soon.' She turned to Jaz and Rory. 'You guys coming to the turtle trek briefing?'

Rory shook his head. 'I promised Dad I'd play a game of pool with him before dinner.'

Bindi nodded. 'Okay. I can always fill you in on what to do if you want to come out with us later.' She turned to Jaz. 'How about you?'

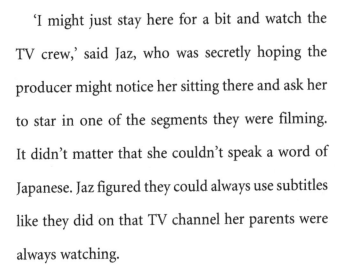

'I might just stay here for a bit and watch the TV crew,' said Jaz, who was secretly hoping the producer might notice her sitting there and ask her to star in one of the segments they were filming. It didn't matter that she couldn't speak a word of Japanese. Jaz figured they could always use subtitles like they did on that TV channel her parents were always watching.

'Looks like it's just you and me then, Jose,' Bindi said. 'I wonder who we're going to get to meet this time?'

A visiting shark expert, a climate-change specialist, a world-famous conservationist – anything was possible on a place like Lady Elliot Island!

CHAPTER EIGHT

JOSIE STARED AT THE TINY

turtle hatchling in Nikki's hand. Perfectly formed, he had black beady eyes and a soft shell. 'Oh, wow, isn't he gorgeous? Can I touch him?'

'Sure,' Nikki told her. 'But be very gentle.'

Josie held out a careful finger and gently stroked

the baby turtle. Turning his head to look at her, he waved his flippers up and down.

'It looks like he's swimming,' Bindi said. 'Clever little hatchling.' She turned to Nikki. 'I'm so glad we got to meet him. Thanks for introducing us. Does he have a name?'

'Not yet,' Nikki said. 'I thought maybe you or one of your friends might like to choose one.'

Bindi smiled at Josie. 'What do you think, Jose? You're good at that sort of stuff.'

'Umm . . . I'm not sure yet. Can I think about it for a while?' she said slowly, relieved that Jaz wasn't there to butt in. Names were important things that said a lot about a person and couldn't be rushed.

'Of course,' Nikki said. 'Don't take too long though. We'll be releasing him –

at least, we think it's a him! – and his little brother or sister on the beach tonight, when the tide changes.'

'There are two hatchlings?' Bindi said. 'Where did you find them?'

'Sarah, my research assistant, found them early this morning when she was out on patrol,' Nikki explained. 'Their mum dug her nest next to some tree roots, and though most of the clutch managed to break out of their shells and get away down the beach, these two somehow got trapped. We were lucky Sarah got there before a gull or other predator found them.'

'How many eggs were in the clutch?' Bindi asked.

'We counted up the broken eggshells and it came to almost a hundred,' Nikki said. 'Including three that didn't hatch at all, and these two that ended up in here.'

'So most of them made it to the ocean?' asked Josie.

'We can't know for sure,' Nikki said. 'But some definitely would have. Although, they don't always head in the right direction, especially if they've been distracted by lights. That's why we ask guests with beachfront cabins to make sure their curtains or shutters are properly closed at night and to turn off all their lights when they leave a room. Otherwise, the hatchlings might head towards the cabin lights rather than towards the shimmer of the ocean in the moonlight.'

She paused for a moment, smiling as she remembered something. 'And sometimes they end up in places they definitely shouldn't. Like what happened last week on the airstrip! I guess they'd mistaken visitors walking with torches for the moon. But don't worry,' she added reassuringly, 'we rescued those little ones as well.'

By now, some of the other guests had turned up for the turtle trek briefing. Nikki popped the hatchling back into a bucket in her office and called everyone over to a large table.

'You'll all need one of these,' she said, handing out a pile of lime-green clipboards. Inside was a map of the island, some photos of different species of turtles, and a series of printed sheets with different sections for guests to fill in. 'Has anyone been turtle trekking before?'

Most of the guests shook their heads.

'Okay, well, this is your chance to experience something really wonderful. It's turtle nesting season at the moment. Every night, female green and loggerhead turtles come up onto the shore to lay their eggs. It's a long process, but if you're prepared to be patient, you can observe the whole thing.' She paused, smiling. 'And you'll be helping me out with my research as well.'

Josie thought this was wonderful. Maybe she wouldn't be a writer after all – studying animals was beginning to sound much more interesting. Or maybe she could combine the two and write books about animals!

'Okay, so here's what you do,' Nikki continued. 'High tide is around 2 am tonight, so the best time to see turtles is an hour either side of that.'

Josie blinked. 2 am? That was the middle of the night! No way would she be able to stay awake until then!

'Don't worry,' Bindi whispered, guessing what was on Josie's mind by the look on her face. 'I'll set an alarm.'

'Go down to the water's edge and look for tracks,' Nikki continued. 'If you see two tracks right next to each other, you're too late. It means the turtle has already laid her eggs and gone back into the water. But if you see only one track, chances are the turtle is still up on the beach.'

'How will we know what the tracks look like?' a woman with a heavy German accent asked.

Nikki held up a large photo of the beach that clearly showed the different sorts of tracks they might find. There were little squiggles and drag marks inside each track, created when a turtle's flippers, belly and tail made contact with the sand.

Once everyone had passed around the photo, Nikki
went on with her briefing.

'Turtles need soft, moist sand to lay their eggs
in, so you won't find any coming up onto parts of
the beach where there's only hard coral. Move very
slowly, and listen for sand being thrown around,
or bits of dry coral clinking together. If you do
hear these noises, sit down on the beach. It means
the turtle is getting ready to dig her nest, and you
don't want her to see you. And, whatever you do,
don't talk to each other in loud voices or use your
torch! The noise and light will disturb the turtle,
and she might turn around and go back into the
ocean.'

'But how will we be able to see?' asked another
woman. 'Aren't we going out in the middle of the
night? It will be too dark.'

'There'll be enough natural light from the moon and the stars,' Nikki assured her. 'Once your eyes adjust, you'll be surprised how much you're able to see.'

For the next ten minutes, Nikki filled everyone in on the different stages of the egg-laying process. First, the turtle would use her flippers to dig a deep hole. After that, she would begin to lay her eggs – up to 120 at a time! Finally, she'd pull sand into the hole with her rear flippers, making sure her precious eggs were completely covered.

'At that stage,' Nikki warned them, 'you need to move inland a bit or you'll get sand in your eyes or get hit by flying coral. It's happened to me, and, trust me, it hurts!'

Josie sat there quietly, drinking it all in. She couldn't believe Jaz had decided to hang around

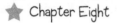

on the beach watching the TV crew rather than come to the briefing – it was all so fascinating. She put up her hand. 'How long does it all take?'

'Anything up to three hours,' Nikki replied. 'Some turtles are slower than others, but it can take up to an hour just for them to fill in the hole.'

'Looks like we won't be getting much sleep tonight,' the German woman joked. 'What about hatchlings? Are we likely to see any of those?'

'You might,' Nikki said. 'The eggs take about 55 days to incubate, and turtle nesting season has been going for a few months now, so it's possible you might see both new eggs being laid and old ones hatching in the same night.'

While Nikki continued to answer questions, Josie crossed her fingers behind her back, wishing and hoping she'd be lucky enough to experience both events. Bindi had told her about the hatch-lings she'd seen the last time the Irwins were on the island. The hatchlings had all joined together and scrambled down to the shore in a group, then swum out into the open ocean to begin their new life. Josie couldn't wait to see it all for herself.

CHAPTER NINE

'DOO DOO DOOOOO! DOO DOO DOOOOO!'

Startled out of a deep sleep, Bindi flung out her arm and scrabbled around until she found the alarm clock under her pillow, then switched it off. Shrieks and screams and a wild chattering

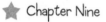

immediately filled her ears, making her think she was back home, listening to all the wild animals at the zoo calling to each other. Confused, she climbed out of her bunk and peered out the window.

But instead of the familiar surrounds of home, she saw a line of spindly trees and, beyond that, waves breaking on a shore lit by silver moonlight. Then she remembered she was on the island and that the shrieks were coming from night birds, not lemurs or trumpeting elephants.

'Is it time to get up?' came a sleepy voice from the other bunk.

'Sure is,' Bindi whispered. 'Careful, we don't want to wake up Robert and Callum.'

Bindi flicked on her pocket torch so they could get changed without needing to turn on the overhead light. Once they were organised, she left the torch on the bedside table, then quietly closed the door behind them. It was a clear night, and the sky was so full of stars they wouldn't need any other light to find their way around.

'Wait here,' she whispered to Josie. 'I'll go and get Jaz and Rory, okay?'

'Fine,' Josie said. 'See you soon.'

Bindi's stomach dropped as soon as she stepped onto the path. Jaz and Rory's cabin was lit up like a Christmas tree! They hadn't even bothered to close the curtains. She'd filled them in at dinner time about how important it was to keep their lights off at night during the turtle nesting season, but they must have forgotten.

'Come in,' Jaz called, when Bindi knocked lightly on the door.

'Hi, it's just me,' Bindi said, opening the door

and taking in the scene inside the cabin. Rory was lying on his bunk with earphones in, and Jaz was reading a book about turtles her mum had bought her from the gift shop. She stepped inside. 'Have you guys slept at all?'

'We didn't think it was worth trying to go to sleep,' Jaz explained, 'so we both just stayed up doing stuff.' She pointed to a wet towel hanging from the end of her bunk. 'Like washing my hair. I love having clean hair.'

The real reason Jaz had washed her hair was so she'd look her best the next day, in case the Japanese TV crew were looking for some local presenters for their animal series. But she was keeping that to herself for now.

'You mean you've had the lights on all this time?' Bindi said, alarmed. The area in front of the cabins was one of the main turtle nesting areas on the island and Nikki had said it was the most likely place to see some turtle action. Three turtles had laid their eggs there the night before, and four the night before that.

Bindi was doubtful that any of the turtles would choose a spot that was so brightly lit – they just wouldn't feel safe. It looked like they'd have to head around to the other side of the island for their turtle trek.

Jaz shrugged. 'Bit hard to read in the dark,' she said, waving her book at Bindi. She put it down on the cupboard, stretched, then gave her brother a light tap on the knee. 'Come on, Rory, it's time to go.'

'Huh?' Rory sat up, a dazed look on his face. Yawning, he pulled his earphones out of his ears, then switched off his phone. 'Must have dozed off,' he

mumbled, reaching for the bottle of mineral water on his bedside table. 'Just give me a minute, okay?'

Bindi sighed. Hadn't he learnt anything while he'd been on the island? There were little signs and messages in all the cabins and common areas encouraging people to act sustainably. Not just by switching off lights and electrical appliances that weren't being used, but things like drinking desalinated water produced on the island rather than packaged water. Rory seemed to be ignoring them all. Bindi noticed that even the bin was full of recyclable products, when there was a recycling bin with clearly labelled compartments only metres from the cabin!

When Rory was finally ready, they made their way to the garden in front of their cabins to collect Josie.

'You okay?' Bindi whispered. 'I'm sorry I was gone so long.'

'I was fine, don't worry,' Josie assured her friend. 'I was checking out all the different stars and constellations. I saw the saucepan, the Southern Cross and the Milky Way – lots of things. You never see this many stars back at home.'

'I know,' Bindi said. 'Mum and I like checking out the night sky too. The stars are so much easier to see out here, away from all the city lights.'

Once they made it down to the beach, Bindi led them across the airstrip towards the other side of the island.

'Whoa, what was that?' Jaz shrieked, as a dark shape flapped past her face.

'Looked like a vampire bat to me,' Rory teased her, 'wanting to make a nest in your hair.'

Jaz shuddered. The thought of a bat – or any kind of creature – becoming entangled in her beautiful hair gave her the heebie-jeebies. 'Thanks a million, Rory,' she sulked. 'You know I don't like bats.'

Josie stifled a smile. 'Are we going to the beach at Coral Gardens?' she asked Bindi, as they turned onto a path near the eastern end of the airstrip.

'Just along from there,' Bindi said, then reminded everyone to keep their voices down now they were getting close to a nesting site.

She led the way across a section of dry hard coral, towards a wider part of the beach where the sand was moist and soft. While they walked, she listened out for digging noises, but the only sound that could be heard was of the waves endlessly lapping the shore.

'Looks like someone else is out too,' Rory said, pointing to a pair of moving lights flashing up and down the beach.

Oh no! Josie groaned, thinking she'd never get to see a turtle now. That was exactly the opposite of what Nikki had told them to do.

They were just rounding a small headland when Bindi held up a hand, signalling everyone to stop. Putting a finger to her lips, she pointed to a section of the beach just above the shoreline.

Josie held her breath. An enormous turtle was using her front flippers to drag herself up the beach. She was well over a metre long, much bigger than the pet turtles some of her friends had.

'It's a turtle! It's a turtle!' Jaz suddenly shrieked, taking a step towards it.

Bindi grabbed her arm, stopping her from

approaching it. 'Jaz!' she whispered urgently. 'Keep your voice down! If you disturb her, she might go back into the ocean.'

'Oops!' Jaz whispered back. 'Sorry, I got carried away. She's just . . . so beautiful. She looks just like the pictures in the book.'

No kidding, thought Josie, hunkering down beside Bindi on the sand. Remembering that Nikki had told them the nesting process could go on for hours, she zipped up her jacket against the chilly night breeze and tried to make herself as comfortable as possible.

'Look,' Bindi whispered a few minutes later. 'It looks like she's getting ready to lay her eggs.'

By now, the turtle had dragged herself all the way to the scrubby trees at the top of the beach, her track marks visible in the moonlight. She was just starting to dig a hole when another light illuminated the sand – the flash from Rory's camera!

'Rory! Noooo!' Bindi's voice came out in a muffled shriek.

But it was too late. Sensing danger, the turtle abandoned her task and slowly lumbered back down to the shore. Slipping quietly into the waves, she headed back to sea.

CHAPTER TEN

THE NEXT MORNING AT breakfast, Josie was still so angry with Rory she could hardly bring herself to speak to him, let alone share a table with him and Jaz. It had taken Bindi's best persuasive skills to finally change her mind and agree to sit down with them.

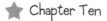

'Come on, Jose,' Bindi said, looking at her friend's untouched plate. 'You have to eat. It's going to be a big day today.'

Josie shook her head. 'I can't stop thinking about that poor turtle. What's going to happen to her babies?'

'She'll be okay,' Bindi reassured her. 'I talked to Mum about it this morning, and she said the turtle probably tried to lay her eggs again once we'd moved on. Or she could have gone to a different spot. Either way, Mum said the nesting process would still happen. Once turtles are ready to lay their eggs, they're ready, if you know what I mean!'

'That's a relief,' Josie said, feeling a bit better. She might not know as much about animals as Bindi and Jaz, but she did know sea turtles were endangered. They needed all the help they could get – not more problems from silly humans with flashing cameras and loud voices.

That left one more problem to deal with . . . Their diving lesson was later that morning, and she still hadn't mastered the art of breathing through her snorkel. Unless she could do this, she'd miss out on all the fun in the water once again.

There were still a couple of spare hours to fill between breakfast and the diving lesson. Hopefully that would be long enough to turn things around. That was, if she could find someone to help her out . . .

'Okay, mask on tight? Mouthpiece resting gently against your teeth? Right, face in the water . . . and breathe!'

It hadn't taken Josie long to find her helper. Within seconds of coming up with her plan, Bindi had offered to take her to the lagoon for some snorkel practice. It was like she could read her mind!

It took a few false starts, and a few bouts of coughing up salty water, but everything finally came together. She was actually breathing through her snorkel!

'I knew you could do it,' Bindi told her. 'You just needed to believe you could. Ready to go look for some turtles?'

'You bet!' Josie said, her eyes sparkling behind her mask.

Bindi pointed to a white buoy floating about 30 metres away. 'Let's head for that buoy. Mum says lots of turtles hang out around there.'

'Sounds awesome!'

Bindi grinned. 'She said to look out for a cheeky one called Terence. He's used to snorkellers coming to visit and loves having his shell stroked.'

I hope he comes for me, thought Josie.

'Right. Remember, if any water enters your snorkel, just blow it out again. And if you need to stop for a while and have a rest, make sure you stand on a sandy part of the reef, rather than on top of live coral. Okay?'

Josie nodded and gave Bindi the thumbs up, then both girls headed for the buoy. Holding her arms in tight by her sides, Josie kicked her legs the way Bindi had shown her, her long fins sending her gliding across the surface of the shallow lagoon. She stared in amazement as a whole new world opened up beneath her. Shoals of colourful fish floated majestically through columns of coral, while anemones waved their delicate arms at her. A bit further ahead, tiny cleaner wrasse fluttered around the lips of a pair of stately Picasso fish. A stripy black and purple creature opened wide, then snapped itself shut as Josie passed over the top of it. She wondered what it was – a clam perhaps? Or a nudibranch?

She was swimming by a chunky outcrop of coral trimmed with shimmering green spikes when something loomed ahead of her like the lamp post in the Narnia books. The buoy! She'd finally reached it.

And then she saw them. First one turtle, then two, their strong flippers powering them along. She couldn't believe how much more graceful they were in the water than on land.

One of the turtles swam towards her, then bobbed away before coming back, like it was playing a game. He swam right up close, then looked her in the eye. This had to be Terence, Josie thought, as she reached down to stroke his tawny shell. Before she knew it, they were swimming together, her arms and legs moving in perfect unison with the turtle's flippers.

Another pair of flippers moved across her line of vision, only these ones were bright blue and attached to feet! It was Bindi, signalling for Josie to follow her.

Bindi led Josie away from the buoy and closer to the shore. As soon as she'd found a sandy place to stand, she pulled her mask and snorkel aside so they could talk, and motioned for Josie to do the same.

'Having fun?'

'Are you kidding? This is *amazing*! No – more than amazing – incredible!' babbled Josie, so excited she could barely get the words out. 'And I saw Terence! We swam together! Did you see him?'

Bindi grinned. 'Sure did. I'm your "snorkel buddy", so I was right beside you the whole way. You were just so spun out by all the things you saw, you didn't notice.'

'Thanks, Bindi. Umm . . . can you be my diving buddy too?'

'Of course!' Bindi laughed. 'I'll be whatever type of buddy you like. All you have to do is ask.' She pulled her mask and snorkel back into place. 'Five more minutes, okay? Then we'd better go and get ready for our diving lesson. No way we're missing out on that!'

CHAPTER ELEVEN

SNUG IN THEIR WETSUITS, BINDI

and Josie sat on the benches outside the Dive Shop, waiting for the rest of the beginner divers to arrive.

'I feel like I should be wearing L-plates,' Josie joked. Although she'd never admit it, she was

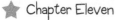

feeling just a tiny bit nervous. Scuba diving was a serious business, and there was just so much to learn.

'You'll be fine,' Bindi told her. 'I thought that on my first dive too.'

Rory arrived next, along with two French girls he'd met at breakfast.

'I think he's a bit keen on them,' Bindi whispered to Josie, watching him practically falling over himself to impress them. 'I didn't know he'd climbed the highest mountain in Australia, put out a raging bushfire with his bare hands or single-handedly saved a small child from being eaten by sharks. Did you?'

'First I've heard of it,' Josie laughed. 'It's the most I've heard him say since we met him.'

Jaz was the last to arrive. 'Sorry I'm late,'

she whispered, squeezing herself onto the bench between Bindi and Josie.

Josie made a show of moving the teensiest bit to the left to make way for her. She was annoyed with Jaz not only for holding everyone up but also because, once again, it seemed she was trying to come between her and Bindi. Feeling she had made her point known, Josie looked to the front, where Pete was patiently waiting to start.

'Good morning, everyone,' he announced in a cheery voice. 'First of all, we need to run through some theory. Then we'll try out what we've learnt here in the pool before finally heading off to the ocean to go diving for real!'

The group spent the next 30 minutes finding out all sorts of things about their bodies they didn't know, like how they contained spaces that needed to be 'equalised' when they were underwater or they'd be in trouble! Equalising seemed pretty simple – all they needed to do was blow gently against their pinched nostrils every metre or so on the way down. Everything would be fine on the way back up, Pete explained, as long as they remembered to keep breathing normally. Holding your breath was a real no-no.

'Everyone got all that?' Pete said at the end. 'Right, let's get you all kitted out in your gear.'

'I feel like the Michelin man,' Josie said, as she practised inflating and deflating her bulky buoyancy vest. 'What's this thing for anyway?'

'It helps keep you afloat in the water,' Pete explained. 'How are you going, Jaz?'

'Fine,' she replied, pulling on a pair of black scuba booties. 'Should I put my fins on now too?'

'Not unless you want to walk around like a duck,' Pete joked, making Josie giggle.

Once everyone was suited up, with their air tanks and dive masks firmly strapped in place, they headed for the pool to begin the second part of the lesson.

Josie listened intently to all the instructions. Pete went through each step slowly and carefully, making sure everyone had mastered it before moving on to the next one. There was a lot to remember! By the time they were up to the part about what to do if the air in your tank ran out, her head was spinning.

Jaz was doing her best to keep up, but her mind kept wandering. While Josie and Bindi were in the lagoon, Jaz and Rory had bumped into the Japanese TV crew in the rec room. She'd found out the crew's schedule for the rest of the day. They had been about to head off to the Bird Rookery to film some of the new chicks and planned to go on a dive boat for the rest of the day. *Their* dive boat. This could be her big chance to get on camera! She'd immediately run back to her cabin and spent the next half-hour practising presenter poses in front of the mirror. That's why she'd been late.

'Jasmine? Jaz? Hellooo?'

Jaz broke out of her daydream to find the rest of the group staring at her. 'Oops, sorry,' she said. 'I was miles away.'

'Can you practise breathing through the regulator underwater for me?' Pete asked.

'Yep, no worries,' Jaz said, making an extra effort to concentrate this time. Bindi gave her the thumbs up as she slowly sank beneath the surface, breathing slowly and steadily into the mouthpiece.

Once Pete was happy that everyone knew how to use the equipment properly, he called them over to the side of the pool for the final part of the lesson.

First, he showed them how to jump safely off the boat and into the water using what he called 'a giant stride'. Next, he showed them how to use hand signals to communicate while underwater. A circle made with your index finger and thumb meant 'okay', and a hand flapping from side to side signalled that something was wrong.

He held up his right hand with the palm facing towards the group. 'What do you think this means?'

'Stop? Or wait?' Bindi suggested.

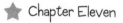

'Exactly,' Pete said, with a nod. 'Okay, how about this one?' he continued, making a fist and pointing his thumb towards the sky.

'Go up?' Josie said.

'Excellent. You're all doing really well.'

Pete ran through the rest of the signals, then asked everyone to choose a dive buddy. 'It's a good idea to choose someone you know well and who you can trust. You need to stick really close to your buddy at all times in case you get into trouble or run out of air. That's probably the most important thing you need to remember.'

He glanced over to the other side of the pool, where Rory was trying to make the French girls laugh with his kangaroo impressions. 'Did you get all that, Rory?'

'Yep,' he said quickly. But the only thing

he remembered from the last ten minutes of instructions was Pete's last sentence. Rory wasn't too worried; he'd had no problems learning how to use the equipment, and surely *that* was the most important thing anyone needed to remember.

'Okay, everyone,' Pete grinned. 'That's a wrap. Enjoy your dive!'

CHAPTER TWELVE

'HEY, BINDI, WANT TO BE MY DIVE buddy?' Jaz asked, as they waded out to the dive boat.

'I'd love to but I already promised Josie,' Bindi told her. 'Maybe we can do something else together later?'

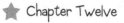

'No worries,' Jaz said sweetly, but inside she was fuming. The TV crew were right behind them. They'd be much more likely to notice her if she was teamed up with someone as famous as Bindi.

'Looks like you're stuck with me, little sis,' Rory said, giving her a friendly nudge.

'Oh, really?' Bindi teased. 'I thought you'd be buddying up with one of your new friends.'

'So did I,' Rory said, puzzled. He was sure the French girls had loved his kangaroo act, especially Monique.

The engine roared to life and the boat took off, heading straight for the Lighthouse Bommies, a popular dive site.

'This is it,' Bindi said, pulling on her fins. 'We're finally going diving!'

'What if I can't remember what to do?' Jaz

stammered, suddenly petrified. 'Or I forget to breathe and my lungs explode?'

'And what if I run out of air?' Josie added. 'Or my mask fogs up and I can't see? Or –'

'Don't worry,' Bindi reassured her friends. 'Nobody's lungs are going to explode. Just stay calm, breathe slowly and evenly like Pete taught us to, and everything will be fine.'

The boat dropped its anchor, and everyone lined up next to the metal platform along its side. One by one, the divers held their masks and regulators firmly in place, then extended their right legs and leapt into the water. They bobbed on the surface for a few moments, then, following Pete's thumbs-down signal, let some air out of their buoyancy vests and slowly submerged themselves.

Once under the water, Bindi stared in

amazement at the canyons of delicate coral below her, and the cavalcade of technicolour marine life darting over and around them. The water here was much deeper than in the lagoon, and she couldn't wait to explore it!

Pete made the 'okay' signal with his forefinger and thumb, and everyone responded with the same.

Except for Rory. Instead of patiently waiting next to his buddy for the next set of instructions, he took off after a white-tip reef shark he'd spotted behind the group.

Bindi's eyes widened. Pete was going to be furious! He'd drummed into them how important it was to never go off on your own while diving.

And she was right. As soon as Pete realised what was happening, he gave everyone the signal to stay with Oko and Chris, the other dive instructors. Then he dashed off after Rory. Pete soon caught up to him and rapped his knuckles on the back of Rory's air tank to get his attention. When that didn't work, Pete grabbed the back of Rory's buoyancy vest, spun Rory around so they were facing each other, then gave him the thumbs-up signal.

Rory stared at Pete, puzzled. The angry expression on the instructor's face didn't match up with the gesture of approval he was giving him. That's what the thumbs-up signal meant, didn't it? That he was doing something good?

Realising that Rory had misunderstood his signal, Pete repeated it. Only this time he used both hands, jerking his fists up and down until Rory finally got the message. Mortified, Rory slowly

ascended to the surface, where Pete helped him back onto the boat.

'Do you have any idea how dangerous that was?' Pete asked him, as soon as they'd both removed their masks. 'Didn't you listen to *anything* I said during the lesson?'

Rory hung his head. 'I guess it was pretty stupid,' he admitted. 'But . . . you know . . . it was a shark! You don't get to see one of those every day.'

'That makes what you did even more dangerous,' Pete said, handing him a dive manual. 'Remember back at the pool this morning when I told you all how important it was to stay next to your buddy? I'm wondering now what other important stuff you might have missed. I think you'd better stay on the boat for a while and read through this.'

Rory stared at him in shock. 'You mean . . . miss out on the rest of the dive?'

Pete shrugged. He didn't want to be too hard on the poor kid. After all, it was only his first dive. And he'd picked up all the technical stuff really well. But Rory also needed to learn how important it was to follow instructions. Especially when you were in a situation where your life could be in danger if you didn't.

'Up to you,' he finally said. 'Take off your scuba gear, read through the manual and we'll give you a test at the end to make sure you know all the rules. If you pass that – and by pass I mean by one hundred per cent – you're back in the water. Sound fair?'

Rory nodded, determined to make things right again. When he thought about it, chasing after a shark alone had been pretty foolish.

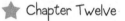

Keeping their arms close to their bodies, Bindi and Josie followed Oko through the water, kicking slowly and evenly from their hips, just like they'd been taught. Any worries Bindi might have felt had melted away as soon as she'd dropped beneath the surface. Her wetsuit kept most of her body warm and dry, and, even though they'd gone down quite deep, she couldn't feel any pressure from the water on her body at all. It was more like flying than swimming.

Shoals of black and yellow striped fish zipped above and around her body, teasing her to follow them. Forests of lime-green algae and seagrass shimmied and waved beneath her, while spiky sea urchins bristled their spines, and black sea cucumbers and bright blue sea stars inched slowly along the ocean floor. She felt just like Alice in an underwater wonderland.

Oko shone a little torch into the crevices of a rock, showing them the different creatures that dwelt there. He pointed out a giant moray eel waiting in the shadows. It was resting now, but Bindi knew that once it was night-time it would emerge from its hidey-hole to grab itself a tasty snack. Everywhere Bindi looked, there was something new and fabulous to see.

When a trickle of water seeped in through the side of her mask, Bindi stopped swimming and snorted through her nose a couple of times to clear it out.

'Okay?' Oko signalled.

Bindi nodded, then remembered that gestures

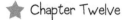

such as nods and shrugs couldn't be recognised underwater. She was just returning the 'okay' signal when she spotted a group of enormous turtles coasting along beneath her, their movements as graceful as ballerinas. One of them broke away from the rest and swam right up to her! It turned its head from side to side, then looked her straight in the eye as if to say, 'Who are you, funny-looking creature, and what are you doing in *my* world?'

Then it was gone – off to the open ocean with its friends. Bindi wished she could follow it, even for just a few moments. What a great life turtles had, she thought, cruising around the world through warm waters, stopping every now and then to visit tropical islands with shimmering lagoons and sandy beaches.

The next thing she knew, Oko was hovering in front of her, giving her the thumbs-up signal. It was time to go back to the boat.

CHAPTER THIRTEEN

BACK ON BOARD, EVERYONE was talking at once.

'Did you see the giant clams opening and closing?'

'And the sea anemones with the little yellow fish hanging around them, just like in *Finding Nemo*?'

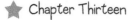

'And that spotty fish with the big lips!'

'And that unicorn fish with the long nose? How weird was that!'

'Not as weird as the manta ray. I thought it was going to swallow me up!'

Pete and Oko exchanged grins. Everyone always carried on like this after their first dive, eager to share all the wonderful things they'd just seen.

The camera crew were keen to film some of them talking about their first scuba diving experience while the boat was still anchored, and – surprise, surprise! – Jaz had been the first to volunteer. Bindi shrugged off her air tank and buoyancy vest, removed her weight belt, then sat down next to Rory.

'Still in trouble?' she asked him.

Rory grinned sheepishly. 'I was, but I think I've

redeemed myself. I read through the manual so many times I'll probably still remember what to do when I'm 50. I passed the test they gave me with flying colours.'

'So it's okay for you to dive now?'

'Yeah, but not till tomorrow. We ran out of time. I did so well in the test, Pete said he'd take me with him on the morning dive and give me a private lesson.'

'Good for –' Bindi began, then stopped as something in the water caught her eye.

'Oh no, look!' she said, pointing to a plastic bag floating on the water. 'There are turtles down there. The ones I saw swam away but it's nesting season, so there are bound to be more.'

Rory looked at her. 'So?'

Bindi realised she'd never got around to having

that talk with Rory. There wasn't enough time to tell him the story of the turtle with the 74 pieces of plastic inside it, but she had to at least let him know that plastic bags and turtles didn't mix.

'Plastic bags look like jellyfish to turtles,' Bindi explained quickly. 'And so they swallow them, and the bags get stuck inside them, and –'

'They die a painful death?' Rory asked. 'I hope not, because there's one heading towards it right now.'

'No!' Bindi gasped, searching for a glimpse of it. 'Where?'

'Down there,' Rory said, pointing to a juvenile green turtle that had come up for air about 20 metres away. It took a breath, dived under, then resurfaced a couple of metres closer to the bag. A few moments later, it dived under again. The next time it came up for a breath, it spotted the bag and headed straight for it.

Bindi made a quick decision. Grabbing Rory's arm, she blurted, 'Tell Pete I'm just going in to grab that bag and I'll be straight back out again.' Then, before Rory or anyone else could stop her, she leapt into the ocean.

Without her buoyancy vest, it was a little harder to stay afloat, but Bindi was a strong swimmer who'd been around water all her life. She knew she'd be okay. And there was no way she could stand by and watch an innocent creature's life in jeopardy, all because someone had been selfish enough to dump their rubbish with no thought for the consequences.

But it was proving to be a bit more difficult than she'd thought. Every time she drew within arm's

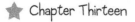

length of the plastic bag, a wave washed it further away from her grasp. She was, however, now much closer to the turtle. Close enough to know that mistaking a plastic bag for a jellyfish was only one of its problems . . .

Josie had been watching Jaz hamming it up for the cameras when Bindi jumped overboard. As soon as she realised what Bindi had done, she rushed to the side of the boat. 'Bindi!' she called. 'What are you doing? Come back!'

By now, everyone else on the boat was calling out to her too.

But instead of answering, Bindi kept swimming.

Confused and worried for her friend, Josie

turned to Rory. 'Did she tell you anything before she jumped?' she asked, her voice shaky.

'It's that plastic bag down there,' Rory told her, pointing to it. 'She's trying to reach it before the turtle does.'

'But she's not trying to reach the bag,' Josie told him, as she watched a choppy wave break over Bindi's head. 'She's trying to reach the turtle. Look! It's moving strangely. There's something wrong with it!'

Bindi stared at the length of fishing line wrapped around the turtle's neck and front right flipper. She'd seen this kind of thing before. Some of the turtles the vets had treated in the Wildlife Hospital at Australia Zoo had been brought in with fishing line wrapped around them, digging into their soft flesh. Though this little turtle could still swim, the line was just tight enough to throw it off balance, which could permanently injure its flipper and make it hard for it to escape from predators or gather enough food to survive. It was clear the turtle needed to be taken onto the boat, so the fishing line could be cut away. Raising her right arm, Bindi signalled for help.

Seconds later, one of the divers leapt overboard and began to swim towards her. Struggling to keep her head above water, Bindi watched the figure approach. *It must be Pete*, she thought, *or maybe Oko*. She could hardly believe her eyes when the diver's head broke clear of the water and she saw who it was.

'Rory?!' she spluttered.

'Don't look so surprised,' Rory laughed. Now that he was up close, he could see why Bindi was so worried about the turtle. 'Oh no! Poor little guy. I think we're going to need more help.'

'Everything okay?' a voice called.

Bindi turned to see Pete and Oko powering towards them.

'It will be soon,' she said gratefully. 'We just need to get this little fella back on the boat.' She grinned. 'And if you've got one of those sharp knives diving instructors always seem to carry around with them, that might come in handy too.'

CHAPTER FOURTEEN

BY DINNER TIME, BINDI WAS THE

talk of the eco-resort. It seemed everyone – guests and staff included – had heard the story of how she'd jumped off a dive boat to save a distressed turtle.

All through the meal, people came over to her

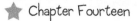

table in twos and threes to congratulate her on her daring feat. The chef had even made her a celebratory cake, with blue icing and green turtles piped around the top. And Robert made a big show of presenting her with a necklace he'd made from sea glass he'd picked up while beachcombing with the Reef Rangers club.

'I was going to save it for your birthday,' he told her. 'But I figured I'd give it to you now instead.'

'Just as well,' Bindi beamed. 'It's a long time to wait until July!' She fastened it around her neck, then flashed him a smile. 'Thanks, little buddy. It's beautiful.'

Bindi was just picking up her fork when one more admirer came to say hello. It was Lani, the little girl from the fish-feeding pool.

'That was really brave of you, Bindi,' Lani

gushed. 'When I get back home, my dad's going to buy me a pet turtle – just a little one I can keep in a tank – and I'm going to name him after *you.*'

'Aw, thanks!' Bindi said. 'But if he's a boy,' she added, with a smile, 'you might be better off calling him Rory. Or, I know, how about Nigel?'

Lani shook her head. 'I like Bindi better.'

Everyone at the table laughed.

'Okay, Bindi, time to fess up,' Josie demanded.

'Yeah,' Jaz said. 'Who – and where! – is this Nigel?'

'Umm . . .' Bindi said, unsure how to break the news to them.

Lani stared at the girls as if they were crazy. 'Nigel's a fish,' she said. 'He's a silver drummer. Nikki told me.'

Josie and Rory burst out laughing.

'A fish?' Jaz muttered, shaking her head.

'Don't blame me,' Bindi chuckled, holding both hands up. 'You're the one who assumed he was a cute guy.'

She watched Lani skip back to her table, then turned to the others, her voice suddenly serious. 'I don't know why everyone's making such a fuss about *me*. After all, Rory, you helped to save the turtle too. And without Pete and Oko, we'd never have got him on the boat.'

'And Pete's knife. Don't forget the important role *it* played,' said a deep voice behind her.

Bindi turned in her seat to see Pete and Nikki standing behind them, grinning.

'How's the little guy doing?' Bindi asked.

'Really well,' Pete told her. 'Fortunately, he

wasn't tangled up too tightly, but it would have got worse the longer it stayed on him, so well done you. We'll pop him in the office overnight just to keep an eye on him. Then, all being well, we'll take him out on the boat with us on the morning dive and release him back into the ocean.'

'Umm . . . Pete?' Rory said.

'Yes, mate?'

'Do you think . . . seeing as I'm coming on the morning dive and everything . . . that I could be the one to put him back in the water?' Rory asked quietly. 'I just want to make sure the water's clear . . . you know, check to see there are no plastic bags or other pieces of rubbish floating around where we let him go.'

Bindi stared at him, stunned. Was this the same Rory who'd whinged about there being no air con or mobile-phone reception, and who threw disposable drink bottles into the bush?

'No worries, mate,' Pete grinned. 'See you here for an early breakfast, okay? Six o'clock sharp,' he added, making Rory groan.

Bindi smiled. Maybe he hadn't changed that much after all.

'Oh, and one more thing,' Pete went on. 'You know that Japanese TV crew that were filming out on the boat today? They took heaps of footage of your rescue effort, Bindi. They want to know if you could do a piece to camera about the dangers of litter in marine environments.'

'Fantastic!' Jaz jumped in quickly. 'I could help you, Bindi. I've got lots of really neat ideas. Why don't you come over to my cabin after dinner so we can discuss them?'

Beside her, Josie arched an eyebrow.

'Umm . . . thanks, Jaz,' Bindi said, her head spinning from all the people she'd spoken to that evening. Presenting on camera was something she could do quite easily – she'd been appearing on TV shows and giving live performances at Australia Zoo for years. But she figured it might be a nice idea to stay behind the scenes for a change and let someone else take the stage.

And she had a very good idea of who that someone should be.

CHAPTER FIFTEEN

AFTER HOURS OF TOSSING AND

turning, Josie finally gave up on trying to sleep. Too many images from the day were running through her mind – shoals of fish, playful turtles and Bindi's leap into the water. And a bossy girl called Jaz, who seemed to be doing her best to come between her and Bindi. She sat up, bumping her head on the bunk above her.

Great. Now everyone else would wake up too, and she didn't feel like talking to *anybody*. But all she could hear was the sound of quiet breathing, with the occasional snort from her brother.

Slipping out of bed, she checked the time on the clock on the bedside table. Almost 4 am. Too early to get up, but too late to get any decent sleep before breakfast.

And then she had a brilliant idea.

She'd head down to the beach and see if she could find any nesting turtles. Only this time, she'd go on her own, without Jaz or Rory there to scare them back into the water.

By the time Josie reached the beach on the other side of the island, the sky was just beginning to lighten. But there were still plenty of stars and Josie knew the sun wouldn't come up for another hour.

Stepping carefully, she moved quietly along the shoreline, searching for tracks. The double track from the night before was still there, along with another set slightly further along. Perhaps the turtle they disturbed had come back after all, once all the noisy humans had left the beach.

And then she saw it; a well-defined single track leading up to the trees at the top of the beach. Holding her breath, Josie delicately made her way across the crunchy coral until she was able to make out a bulky oval object on the sand.

Seconds later, a pile of sand and broken coral went flying through the air. Josie tried to remember what Nikki had told them about the various nesting stages. The turtle might be covering her eggs, which meant the process was nearly over. Or she might be digging out the body pit, which meant it was only just beginning. There was only one way to find out! As quietly as she could, Josie edged a little closer to the turtle, trying to get a better look.

The sky lightened a little more, revealing a hole that was definitely being dug out, rather than filled in. Yes! She'd arrived just in time. Josie sat down on the beach, hugging her knees, waiting for the show to start. It was going to be fantastic! Not only that, she was going to have the whole experience to herself, without having to listen to Jaz go on and on about how much she knew about animals.

Thirty seconds later, guilt set in. Josie thought about how disappointed Bindi would be when she found out she had been lucky enough to see a nesting turtle. She thought about Jaz and Rory too. Sure, Jaz was annoying, but she was also passionate about animals in her own irritating way. And there was no way someone who loved animals could be all bad.

Josie checked her watch. About half an hour had passed. Nikki had told them the nesting process could take anything up to three hours. If she hurried, she might be able to make it up to the cabins and back to the beach in time to see the turtle lay her eggs.

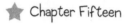

Josie had only gone a few metres along the beach when she heard the crunch of coral behind her. Whipping around, she came face-to-face with . . .

'Bindi! How did you know to come?' Josie cried. 'Quick, come and sit down over here. The turtle's about to dig her egg chamber. She'll be laying her eggs any minute.'

Bindi grinned. 'I've been right behind you the whole time, Jose.'

Josie wrinkled her forehead, puzzled. 'You have? But where?'

'You didn't think I'd let you go off in the dark on your own, did you? I heard you get up and followed you down to the beach.' She giggled. 'I had to dodge a few low-flying vampire bats and flesh-eating geckos on the way though.'

Josie bit her lip, feeling guilty again for ever doubting their friendship.

'It's not like you to go off on your own like this,' Bindi said gently. 'You're the most fun person I know, always happy and positive. Want to tell me what's wrong?'

Josie wasn't sure where to start. How could you tell a best friend you were jealous of her friendship with someone else? Or that her new friend made you feel like you weren't worth hanging out with?

'Come here,' Bindi said, pulling Josie into a warm bear hug. 'It's something to do with Jaz, isn't it?'

Josie nodded.

'She can be a bit full-on at times,' Bindi responded, 'but her heart is in the right place. Sure, Jaz is my friend too, but just because I like her, it doesn't mean I like you any less.'

Bindi gave Josie one of her special boa-constrictor squeezes, making her friend giggle. 'Just remember, you're my best bud and you always will be. Come on, let's go and get the others before Mama Turtle here heads back into the ocean for another 30 years!'

CHAPTER SIXTEEN

BINDI AND HER FRIENDS SAT ON

the beach, mesmerised by what they'd just seen. Once she'd decided her egg chamber was deep enough, the turtle had laid 104 leathery eggs, each the size of a ping-pong ball. They'd counted each one as it came out.

Then, remembering Nikki's advice, they'd stood well away from the pit while the turtle kicked up a storm, using her powerful back flippers to flick sand and coral over the eggs. One day soon, in about two months' time, each of those tiny eggs would release a hatchling, and they would all go scrambling down the beach to the water to start their new life in the world.

And then, if they were lucky, some of those hatchlings would grow up and have babies of their own. And because turtles live for many, many years, some of them might even get to swim with the next generation of kids that came to the island!

'It's a pity we didn't get to see any hatchlings ourselves,' Josie said, just as the sun came up across the water.

'I know,' Bindi said. 'I really wanted to see them too. But never mind, there's always next year. Let's make a vow to all come back to the island in February.' She grinned. 'Or maybe it would be better if we came in July . . .'

'Isn't that when the whales come past?' Josie asked.

'Sure is,' Bindi said, her smile as wide as the shoreline. 'But it's also my birthday, remember!'

Josie laughed. 'Hey, that reminds me of something. Remember the two little hatchlings Nikki was looking after in the office? We never got around to naming them for her.'

'Why don't we do it now?' Bindi suggested. 'We can tell her at breakfast.'

'I've got a good idea,' said Jaz. 'How about . . . Princess Jasmine!'

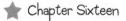

Rory rolled his eyes. 'How about *not* that. I vote we call them . . . Arthur and Martha!'

'What?' he said, when Jaz threw sand at him. 'So it's okay to call a fish Nigel, and a turtle Terence, but I can't call a couple of baby turtles Arthur and Martha?'

'Sounds like a bonza idea to me!' Bindi said. 'Arthur and Martha it is. Come on, let's get some breakfast before the dive team get there and demolish it all!'

CHAPTER SEVENTEEN

ON THE LAST NIGHT OF THEIR

stay, the Japanese camera crew took over the rec

room to shoot the final scenes for their TV series.

Afterwards, they were planning to throw a huge

party for all the guests, where they were going

to screen the 'rushes' – rough cuts of each day's

filming – of the show. Everyone was hanging out to see if they'd scored a part in one of the segments.

Hiro, the lighting guy, set up a bank of lights where the pool table used to be, while Masaki, the cameraman, fiddled with a bunch of camera lenses and the production assistants, Kaori and Keiko, ran around with clipboards, checking things.

Bindi had managed to convince the producer to let her and her friends watch the segment from the back of the room, on the condition that they promised not to talk while the camera was rolling. She pulled four chairs together for them to sit on – although one of them wasn't going to be getting much use from the star of the show.

'Quiet on the floor, please!' the director announced.

Keiko led out what TV people liked to call 'the

talent' to the middle of the room. 'Stand on this cross, please,' she requested. 'And speak into that camera over there.'

Bindi sat quietly, waiting for the segment to start. She had absolutely no doubt it was going to go really, really well.

'And . . . action!'

'So, this week, I found out something really important that I'd like to share with you all,' Rory began, his voice a little shaky at first, though it soon settled down. 'This is pretty embarrassing to admit, but a few days ago, like thousands of other thoughtless people around the world, I tossed a plastic bottle away without stopping to consider the consequences.

'Fortunately, due to the actions of my sister and new friends, this bottle ended up in the proper place for it – a recycling bin. Sadly, though, many of the plastic bottles and bags dumped by people end up in waterways and make their way to our oceans, where they become a danger to marine animals such as the turtles found here at Lady Elliot Island.

'To a turtle, a plastic bag floating on the surface of the water looks just like a jellyfish – one of their favourite foods. But if they swallow it, it can block their digestive system and kill them.'

Rory paused, looking like he'd forgotten the next part of his speech. Bindi shot him a big smile of encouragement, and he gathered his thoughts and continued.

'Did you know that one trillion plastic bags are produced around the world every year? So if only a tiny percentage of those end up in the ocean, it's still far too many. An American scientist counted 76 plastic bags floating in the water around his research boat in just one minute! A Minke whale stranded on a beach in France had nearly a kilogram of plastic in its stomach! And it is estimated that one million birds and 100,000 sea creatures – including turtles – die every year after swallowing plastic or getting tangled in it, just like our little friend was this week.

'So, what can we do to help? Well, there are lots of things. First, we can stop using so much plastic. Use reusable shopping bags and bottles instead of getting new ones every time. Take your lunch to school or work in a paper bag or your own reusable container. Buy food in bulk to cut down on packaging. But, most of all, don't be a Waste Wally, like I was. Be a Wildlife Warrior instead.'

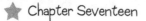

Rory turned to the producer. 'Um, I think that's it.'

'Woo hoo! Way to go!' Bindi called, forgetting she'd promised not to make any noise while the camera was still rolling. 'Whoops, sorry,' she whispered.

'Don't worry,' Keiko told her. 'We can edit that bit out later.'

Jaz stared at her brother, amazed. 'How did you know all that stuff?'

Rory shrugged. 'The internet, mostly. I promised Dad I'd mow the lawn for the next six months if he bought me some internet vouchers. I was going to offer to wash his car too, but then I remembered about water restrictions. Plus, why waste water when you can leave your car out in the rain to get clean for free?'

'Is this the real Rory?' Jaz teased, pinching his arm. 'Or have aliens swapped him overnight?'

Rory rolled his eyes. 'Hands off,' he warned her. 'And then Bindi helped with information, of course. *I* put it all together though,' he insisted.

'You definitely did,' Bindi said, delighted with the progress her new Wildlife Warrior recruit had made in the short space of a week. Whether it be whale-watching or turtle-nesting season – it didn't really matter! – Bindi couldn't wait till the next time her fabulous buddies all got to meet up again.

SEA TURTLES

Sea turtles have been roaming the oceans for more than 100 million years. All of the eight species are classified as endangered. Out of every thousand little turtles that hatch, only one will make it to adulthood.

In 2009, Australia Zoo launched a Turtle Research Project. Rafael, a loggerhead turtle, was rescued after he was found with a crab-pot float line entangled around his neck and flipper. After treatment at the Australia Zoo Wildlife Hospital, Bindi released him back into the ocean from the zoo's research vessel, *Croc One*. His progress, along with other sea turtles, is being tracked by satellite, and the data collected will be used to help the conservation effort for turtles around the world.

To find out more about the protection of Australian wildlife, please visit:

www.wildlifewarriors.org.au

Keep a lookout for the next two books in the

Bindi Behind the Scenes series

BOUNCING OFF THE MENU

and

A GHOSTLY TALE

Publishing October 2012